MUHAMMAD ★ ALI ★

THE MAN WHO COULD

FLOAT LIKE A BUTTERFLY

AND STING LIKE A BEE

story by **NTOZAKE SHANGE** | illustrated by **EDEL RODRIGUEZ**

DISNEY **JUMP AT THE SUN** **LOS ANGELES** **NEW YORK**

When I first met Muhammad Ali, I was just beyond my childhood. I believed in heroes. I believed in him. What struck me most were his hands. They were bigger than my father's hands, even bigger than my grandfather's hands that were shaped like large gourds from years and years of farming. But even the size of Ali's hands wasn't as astonishing as his very person. With me he was soft-spoken and gentle. At a time when some black people were afraid to look white people in the eye, I knew that Muhammad Ali looked white folks straight in the face and dared them to say anything about how pretty he was, how invincible and independent. Some wanted to diminish him and call him Cassius Clay, even though he had announced to the whole world that he was Muhammad Ali: he wasn't Cassius Anybody anymore. I was proud when he took up with the Nation of Islam and refused to fight in Vietnam. At a time when almost no one was protesting the war, Muhammad Ali took a stand. As a result, his boxing license was revoked without due process or a hearing. While his lawyers appealed his case, he struggled without a way to make a living. Dr. King was virtually the only public figure to openly support his decision. Then the Supreme Court unanimously overturned the ruling. **Muhammad Ali gave me hope and courage. He still does.**

—Ntozake Shange

With special thanks to my editor, Maureen Sullivan—N.S.

With special thanks to the Kenol family—E.R.

Text copyright © 2002 by Ntozake Shange
Illustrations copyright © 2002 by Edel Rodriguez

Printed in the United States of America
FAC-034274-17111
This book is set in ITC Franklin Gothic / Adobe.

The artwork was prepared using pastel, gouache, and spray paint on colored papers
with monoprinted woodblock ink line.

First Edition, October 2002
Second Edition, June 2017
10 9 8 7 6 5 4 3 2 1
Library of Congress Cataloging-in-Publication Data on file.
ISBN 978-1-368-00827-3

Visit www.jumpatthesun.com

To my dad, Paul T. Williams, with love—N.S.

For Steven, Kevin, and Bryan—E.R.

★ HE WAS ★

CASSIUS CLAY

BORN AND RAISED IN

LOUISVILLE

KENTUCKY

As a boy,
he struggled to make his way
in the segregated world of the
**PRE–CIVIL RIGHTS
SOUTH.**

Cassius believed
in a colored
SUPERMAN.

★ ★ ★ ★ ★

"Mama, I don't tell stories.
I tell the truth.
If there's a white
SUPERMAN,
then there's gotta be
A COLORED ONE.
Makes common sense to me."

He loved the
power of
WORDS.

★ ★ ★ ★ ★

"Cassius, without you
to help me with the rhymes,
I wouldn't have the
best-selling signs in town,"
said Pa.
" 'COME ON IN
FOR A SHAVE AND
A TRIM'?
That's nothing, Pa! I can rhyme
all the time!" said Cassius.

He knew things were hard for his people.
His parents helped him see a different way.
"Mama, is **HEAVEN** divided up like Louisville, with
White and Colored, and are the Negroes in heaven poor like
the ones livin' in Smoketown?"
**"OH, BABY. THE LORD LOVES
ALL HIS CHILDREN.**
It's people what mess up what the Lord's work is.
So long as you are alive, I want you to remember,
YOU ARE GOD'S WORK."

Most of all, Cassius knew that
FREEDOM was worth fighting for.
And to Cassius when he was a boy, freedom was a brand-new bike.

"Somebody stole my bike, and I'm gonna whup 'em **GOOD.**"

"I'm gonna have to be the best fighter there is, 'cause nobody's gonna take nothin' else **FROM ME AND MINE.**"

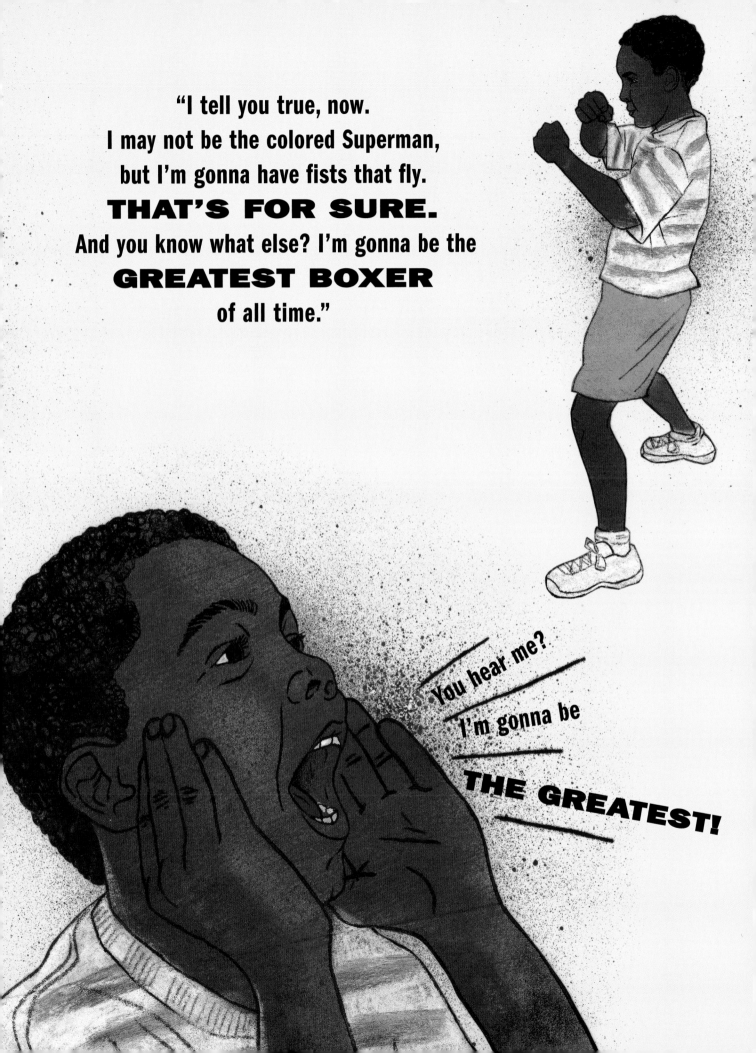

Early on, Cassius developed his famous style. Lightning-quick on his toes, brave, cool, and disciplined, he would duck and bob his way around the ring, exhausting his opponent, waiting to strike. The hard work began to pay off. Cassius won the gold medal at the

1960 OLYMPICS.

He was eighteen years old.

He believed in
EXCELLENCE.

Four years later, Cassius Clay became the **HEAVYWEIGHT CHAMPION OF THE WORLD** in a bout against Sonny Liston. Clay had come into his own. He embraced Islam as his new faith, and took a new name—Muhammad Ali. In 1965 he fought Liston again, knocking him out in one round to retain his title. Then the title he had worked so hard for was stripped away because he refused to fight in **VIETNAM**.

A deeply religious man, he believed in **EQUAL RIGHTS** for all people.

When it came to fighting, he knew he was **GOOD.**
"I'm MUHAMMAD ALI.
I float like a butterfly
AND STING LIKE A BEE.
There's nobody bigger or better than me."

But in 1971, Ali suffered a tremendous defeat
to Joe Frazier in the "Fight of the Century."
He didn't give up. Three years later, after intense training,
he regained the title of **HEAVYWEIGHT
CHAMPION OF THE WORLD**
in eight brutal rounds against George Foreman in Zaire
in what became known as "The Rumble in the Jungle."

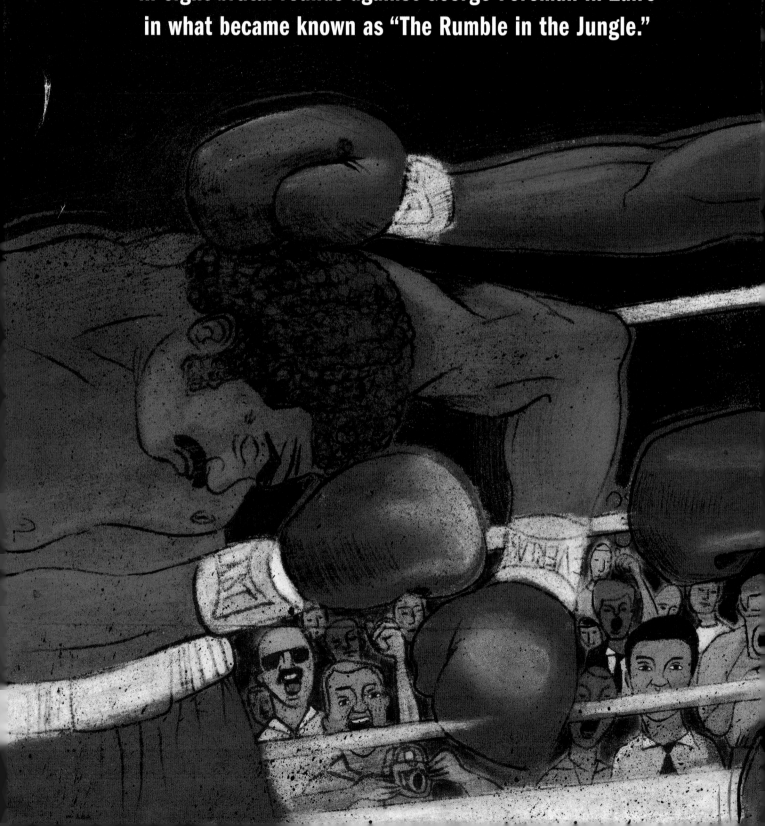

He is a
HERO
for all time.

FORGET THE REST
'CAUSE HERE I AM

THE GREATEST
THE BEST

THE HEAVYWEIGHT
CHAMPION
OF THE WORLD

ALI!

IMPORTANT DATES

January 17, 1942: Cassius Marcellus Clay, Jr., is born in Louisville, Kentucky. His father, Cassius Clay, Sr., is a sign painter. His mother is a part-time domestic.

1954: Cassius Clay's bike is stolen, and he reports it missing to police officer Joe Martin, who suggests that before Cassius threatens to beat someone up, he ought to learn how to fight. Cassius begins training with Martin at the

Columbia Gym. Joe Martin later says that Cassius is the most dedicated and determined boxer he has ever seen.

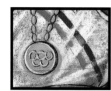

1960: Clay wins Olympic Gold Medal in Rome.

1964: In February, Clay wins World Heavyweight title in a fight against Sonny Liston. Days later, his conversion to Islam, and his new name, Muhammad Ali, become public knowledge.

1965—67: Ali wins nine more fights, seven by knockouts. He retains his World Heavyweight title.

February 1966: Ali is classified 1-A by the draft board. A deeply religious man, he asks to be classified as a conscientious objector.

April 28, 1967: The Army refuses to accept Ali's request to be classified as a conscientious objector. When Ali refuses to be inducted into the Army, his heavyweight championship title is taken away by the World Boxing Association. After a two-day trial, he is given the maximum sentence of five years imprisonment, released pending an appeal of the case, and fined $10,000. Every state revokes his boxing license.

1968—69: Ali briefly retires from boxing.

October 26, 1970: Ali comes back to boxing, beating Jerry Quarry in three rounds with a knockout.

March 8, 1971: In "The Fight of the Century," Ali goes fifteen rounds against Joe Frazier, and is defeated, losing the World Heavyweight Championship.

June 28, 1971: The Supreme Court of the United States unanimously reverses Ali's conviction for refusing induction in the Army.

October 30, 1974: In "The Rumble in the Jungle" in Zaire, Africa, Ali knocks out George Foreman and regains the World Heavyweight Championship title.

February 15, 1978: After defending the title successfully nine times, Ali loses his Heavyweight title to Leon Spinks.

September 15, 1978: Ali faces Leon Spinks again, and this time wins, becoming the first boxer in history to win the World Heavyweight title three times.

1979: Ali announces his retirement.

October 2, 1980: Ali comes back to boxing, and loses to Larry Holmes.

December 11, 1981: Ali fights his last fight in Nassau, Bahamas. He loses to Trevor Berbick, and retires from boxing.

Summer Olympics, 1996: Ali, suffering from Parkinson's disease, lights the Olympic torch at the opening of the Olympic Games, in Atlanta, Georgia.

June 3, 2016: Ali dies at the age of seventy-four.

Additional Resources:

Conklin, Thomas. *Muhammad Ali: The Fight for Respect.* Brookfield, CT: Millbrook
  Press, 1994.

Freedman, Suzanne. *Clay vs. United States: Muhammad Ali Objects to War,*
  Landmark Supreme Court Cases. New York: Enslow, 1997.

Haskins, Jim. *Champion: The Story of Muhammad Ali.* New York: Walker Books, 2002.

Myers, Walter Dean. *The Greatest: Muhammad Ali.* New York: Scholastic, 2001.

Tessitore, John. *Muhammad Ali: The World's Champion, Impact Biography.*
  New York: Franklin Watts, 1998.